THE WILD BABY

by BARBRO LINDGREN

pictures by EVA ERIKSSON

adapted from the Swedish by JACK PRELUTSKY

The Wild Baby

SCHOLASTIC INC.

ISBN 0-590-33363-1

Swedish text copyright © 1980 by Barbro Lindgren. Illustrations copyright © 1980 by Eva Eriksson.
English text copyright © 1981 by Jack Prelutsky. All rights reserved.
This edition published by Scholastic Inc., 730 Broadway, New York, NY 10003,
by arrangement with Greenwillow Books. Swedish edition entitled
Mamman och den vilda Bebin published by Raben & Sjögren.

12 11 10 9 8 7 6 5 4 3 2 1   9   4 5 6 7 8 9 / 8

Printed in the U.S.A.   09

Mama loved her baby Ben,
her small and precious child,
but he always disobeyed her,
he was reckless, loud and wild.

He disappeared one morning
when he should have been in bed.

She found him sleeping soundly
in the wooden clock instead.

He crept into her room one night,
she snored and didn't hear,
and softly as the slyest cat
he climbed the chandelier.
He dangled there until it broke,
then hurried out as mama woke.

He fell into the toilet bowl
and so he had to shout,
"Mama! Hurry! Help! I'm stuck!
Please mama! Get me out!"
Mama rushed in, terrified,
and quickly pulled him back outside.

He clambered up the kitchen sink
and dove in for a swim.
He broke a lot of dishes,
mama really scolded him.
"How come you never let me play!"
he grumbled as he stormed away.

He crawled into a big blue sack
and left without a sound,
poor mama hunted vainly,
baby Ben could not be found.

But late that night, the big blue sack
marched right into the hall.
"Hello!" said baby Ben, "I'm back!"
She hugged him, sack and all.

She took him out to get some air,
but all at once he wasn't there.
She shuddered as a car sped by,
and surely was about to cry.

But then she spied him in a tree,
relaxing on a limb,
she sat below, so when he fell,
she softly cushioned him.

Soon afterward, at lunchtime,
baby Ben grew very ill.

He had spots and dots all over,
with a fever and a chill.

So mama put her Ben to bed,
she held his hand, she stroked his head,
she kissed his nose, she rubbed his ears,
he soon was well, she dried her tears.

What happy noises then they made,
as all that night they danced and played.

One day she took him for a stroll,
they walked and walked for hours,
and when they reached a grassy knoll,
she stooped to gather flowers.
But as she picked a small bouquet,
he tiptoed off and slipped away.

When mama saw he wasn't there,
the tears streamed down her face,
she wept and wept in great despair.
"He's gone without a trace.
I'll never find him in the wood,
my baby Ben is lost for good."

Then suddenly, out popped his head,
"A wolf just licked my face," he said.

"I licked him back, he ran away,
 we won't *see* *him* again today."
Mama broke into a smile
and hugged him tightly for a while.
She bundled home her baby Ben....

Of course, he's since run off again.